The Missing Wedding featuring Barbie™

By Karen Krugman
Illustrated by Laura Westlake

A GOLDEN BOOK • NEW YORK
Western Publishing Company, Inc., Racine, Wisconsin 53404

It was a lovely summer morning. Barbie and Skipper were busy decorating their house.

"Be careful with those glass bowls!" warned Barbie.

"I'm being *very* careful," Skipper promised.

"I guess I'm a little nervous," Barbie admitted. "I want everything to be perfect for Tracy and Todd's wedding."

"The house looks beautiful," Skipper reassured Barbie. "Now it's time for us to get ready, too."

Barbie and Skipper put on their gowns. "I love being the flower girl," giggled Skipper.

"And I'm proud to be the maid of honor," said Barbie. "Let's pick up our bride."

"I'm so excited!" Tracy said when the girls arrived. "Can you help me get dressed?"

Very carefully, Barbie buttoned all the tiny buttons on Tracy's wedding gown.

"You're the loveliest bride in the world," Barbie said softly.

Just then Barbie's cat, Fluff, scampered into the room, followed by Skipper. "Fluff must have sneaked into the car," Skipper said breathlessly. "Don't worry. I'll catch her."

Skipper leaped at Fluff and landed on Tracy's dress. With a *r-r-r-ip*, the train tore off!

"I'm so sorry," Skipper moaned, horrified.

Tracy picked up her tattered train. "What'll I do?" she wailed.

"Take off your dress and put it in the box," Barbie said to Tracy. "I'm sure the dressmaker can fix it."

When the dressmaker saw the gown, she said, "Oh, yes. I can fix this."

Finally she snipped off the last thread. "Your wedding dress is just fine now," she said to Tracy.

Tracy sighed with relief and tucked the gown into the box.

Barbie had one last errand to do. Skipper and Tracy
waited while Barbie picked up her shoes for the wedding.
"They're perfect," Barbie said. "Now we can relax and
enjoy the wedding."
Tracy held the box tightly and headed for the car.

"Wait a second!" said Barbie. "Maybe I'm imagining it, but that box looked a lot bigger before."

Quickly, Tracy opened the box. Inside she found six pairs of bright-blue jogging shoes. "Oh, no!" she cried. "My box got switched at the shoe store!"

Barbie rushed back into the store. "Did you see someone leave with a big box?" she asked the salesman.

"Yes," the salesman replied. "A woman did leave here carrying a big box. I noticed her because she wore a floppy straw hat."

"Thanks!" said Barbie.

Outside, a postman was delivering mail. "Did you see a woman carrying a box and wearing a floppy straw hat?" Barbie asked.

"I sure did," said the postman. "She drove off in a red van that had the word FLO printed on it."

"I've got to find her!" said Barbie.

Barbie got back into her car. "I know who has your dress," she told Tracy. "A woman driving a red van that says FLO on it."

"There's a red van!" Skipper shouted.

Barbie chased the van until it came to a stop in front of a car wash.

Four firemen got out of the van and began washing cars.

"We're washing cars to raise money for the fire department," the captain explained.

CAR WASH

Barbie sighed. "I guess you haven't seen a red van with the word FLO on it."

"I just washed a red van," said the captain. "It headed toward Main Street."

"This is turning into a wild dress chase," moaned Tracy.

Tracy spotted a van on Main Street. "There it is!" she cried. The van said: FLO'S FISH STORE.

Did you buy some shoes today?" Barbie asked the driver.

"Shoes?" he said. "My wife Flo and I spent all morning delivering fish."

Tracy burst into tears. "We'll *never* find my dress!"

On the sidewalk, Skipper bought a bouquet for Tracy. "This is for you," she said. "If I hadn't tripped on your train, we wouldn't be in this mess."

"Flowers are everywhere today," Barbie said. "A lady's even putting flowers on the lampposts. And she's wearing a floppy straw hat!"

Barbie hurried over to the woman. Her heart was pounding hard as she asked, "Did you buy any shoes today?"

The woman looked surprised. "Sure. I bought six pairs of jogging shoes for my children."

"Hurray!" yelled Skipper. "We found her!"

"Our boxes were switched at the shoe store," Barbie explained. "You got Tracy's wedding dress, and she got your jogging shoes."

The woman led them to a parking lot. There was the red van. It said FLOWERS, and all the letters except F, L, and O were faded.

"I knew it!" Barbie said. "FLO is short for FLOWERS."

Back at Barbie's house, Skipper was arranging chairs in the living room. Soon Todd and Ken arrived on Ken's motorbike.

"Would you believe my car broke down?" Ken asked.

Barbie laughed. "Today I'd believe *anything*!"

Barbie and Skipper went upstairs to help Tracy dress.
"This antique locket is *something old*," said Barbie.
"My dress is *something new*," said Tracy.
"My comb can be *something borrowed*," said Barbie.
"But where's *something blue*?" wondered Skipper.
Suddenly, Tracy's veil seemed to leap off the bed!

Skipper caught it. "It's Fluff!" Skipper groaned. "She's up to more mischief. Hey! Let's use Fluff's bow for *something blue*."

"That's a great idea, Skipper," Barbie said happily.

Barbie tied Fluff's bow around Tracy's bouquet.

When all the guests had arrived, the ceremony began.
"Weddings are wonderful," sighed Barbie.
"*This* wedding is especially wonderful," whispered
Skipper. "I'm so relieved it worked out!"
Barbie squeezed Skipper's hand as the bride and groom
kissed.

After the ceremony, everyone went
into the garden to pose for pictures.

"Watch out for Fluff!" warned Skipper.
    "Let's keep Fluff in the picture," said Tracy.
"She's certainly been an important part of
my wedding!"

When it was time for Tracy and Todd to leave for their honeymoon, Tracy called, "Get ready to catch my bouquet!"

All the girls gathered around.

"Here it comes!"

The lucky girl who caught the bouquet was Tracy's very best friend—Barbie!